With special thanks to Michael Ford

www.seaquestbooks.co.uk

ORCHARD BOOKS
338 Euston Road, London NW1 3BH
Orchard Books Australia
Level 17/207 Kent St, Sydney, NSW 2000

A Paperback Original
First published in Great Britain in 2013

Sea Quest is a registered trademark of Beast Quest Limited
Series created by Beast Quest Limited, London

Text © Beast Quest Limited 2013
Cover and inside illustrations by Artful Doodlers,
with special thanks to Bob and Justin © Orchard Books 2013

A CIP catalogue record for this book is available from
the British Library.

ISBN 978 1 40831 851 5

1 3 5 7 9 10 8 6 4 2

Printed and bound by CPI Group (UK) Ltd, Croydon, CR0 4YY

The paper and board used in this paperback are natural recyclable
products made from wood grown in sustainable forests. The
manufacturing processes conform to the environmental regulations of
the country of origin.

Orchard Books is a division of Hachette Children's Books,
an Hachette UK company

www.hachette.co.uk

KRAYA
THE BLOOD SHARK

BY ADAM BLADE

ORCHARD

TEN YEARS EARLIER . . .

>LEAPING DOLPHIN, DIVELOG ENTRY 176.43

LOG BY: Niobe North
MISSION: Find the legendary city
            of Sumara
LOCATION: 1,603 fathoms deep.
            Co-ordinates unknown.

We don't have much time. This may be
the last entry I make. We're stuck
on the ocean bed and both engines
have failed.

The *Leaping Dolphin* is surrounded by
ocean crawlers. Hundreds of them.
They're attacking. They're scraping
at the hull. It's only a matter of
time before they break through.
Unless Dedrick can get the engines
started again, it's the end.

If this tape is ever found — if it
ever reaches you, Callum, and Max —
I want you to know I love you, and

>LOG ENTRY ENDS

CHAPTER ONE

THE FINAL FIGHT

The ocean currents tickled Max's skin like an autumn breeze. He shivered and tightened his grip on the aquabike's handles. The bike's thermometer reading was dipping more the further north they travelled, but that wasn't the only thing making him jittery. Every mile they went was a mile closer to the Black Caves and their enemy, the Professor.

Closer to my dad, too, thought Max.

The Professor had kidnapped his father, Callum, from Aquora City. According to Max's Merryn friend, Lia, the Professor was collecting experts to help build weaponry. So it made sense for him to take Max's dad, who was Head Defence Engineer of Aquora. Max just couldn't work out how the Professor had found Callum in the first place.

I won't lose both my parents to the sea, he thought.

Max's mum had disappeared on a voyage years before with her brother. They had been looking for Sumara, the city of the Merryn – a legendary race of underwater beings. But neither had ever come back. Just two more explorers lost in the perilous oceans of Nemos.

Silt danced in the water ahead, so Max switched on the headlights. The beams caught Spike's flashing tail as the swordfish swam through the water with Lia on his back. No, the Merryn were definitely not just a legend. Lia glared back, her eyes wide, and her silver hair billowing like a cloud.

"You may as well announce to everyone that we're coming!" she said.

Max dipped the beams, twisted the throttle and drew up alongside her. His dogbot, Rivet, followed with a pulse of his propeller.

"Sorry," Max said to the Merryn princess. "I'm still learning, I guess."

Lia scanned the sea ahead. "I've never been this far from home before. I can sense something out there."

"Tell me about it," Max replied, nervously patting the harpoon gun strapped to the side of the bike.

They had travelled miles from Sumara, where Lia's father ruled. They were even further from Aquora City, where Max had grown up with his dad. It seemed a lifetime since he'd first ventured into the ocean after the Professor's evil Cyber Squid. Max had nearly drowned, and it was only Lia's Merryn Touch that had saved his life. His fingers searched his neck for the gills she'd given him. It was still hard to believe he could breathe underwater without a diving suit.

Max reached out to rub Rivet's metal head. "I can't help thinking we could be heading into a trap."

Lia shrugged. "I don't think we have a choice. We have to track down the Professor."

As well as snatching Max's dad, the Professor had stolen the Skull of Thallos from the Merryn city of Sumara. Without it, the Merryn had lost their powers to control the seas, which meant they were all in danger. The Professor was using the Skull fragments and state-of-the-art technology to control giant beasts of the ocean, turning them into vicious fighting machines. Max and Lia had liberated three Robobeasts and recovered three fragments of the Skull – but each battle had been more deadly than the one before.

"You're shivering," said Lia. "Hang on a moment. I know what you need to warm up."

She leant forward and whispered close to Spike's head. The swordfish dipped his sharp nose and dived. The dark water swallowed Lia up. Max waited, glad he had Rivet's red eyes and flashing lights to keep him company. He wondered whether he'd ever get the chance to confront the Professor face to face. Lia's Merryn cousin, Glave, had told them a terrible Robobeast guarded the Black Caves – Kraya the Blood Shark. Even the name was frightening enough to make Max want to turn back.

Lia emerged from the sea floor, trailing what looked like a rug in her hand. She slipped off Spike's back and held it out. "Put this on," she said.

Now that she was closer Max realised it was a blanket of waving orange tendrils. Lia had torn two armholes in it.

"What is it?" asked Max.

"Fur-weed," said Lia. "We make blankets out of it for Merryn tadpoles."

"Tadpoles?"

"Our young," she said. "You know, hatchlings?"

Max slipped on the vest and instantly

felt warmer. "You come from eggs?"

Lia frowned. "Of course. How are Breathers born? Do you fall out of the sky?"

Max grinned. "Never mind. Shall we check the Skull for directions?"

"Let's keep moving," Lia replied. "I don't like it here."

They swam on through the murk. Gradually the water became clear enough for Max to switch off his bike's lights completely. The ocean floor stretched for miles on all sides, completely flat and bare but for a few pebbles and scraps of dying weed. The water was empty of fish or any other marine life.

Max felt more relaxed now that he could see further. "Let's stop here," he said. Lia nodded and slid off her swordfish.

Rivet was obviously glad to be out of the murky patch too, and nosed playfully around Spike's belly, until the swordfish gave him a whack with his tail and darted off to scour the seabed.

"Here, boy!" Max beckoned to the dogbot and Rivet swam over.

"Fish hit me, Max," he barked.

"You asked for it," said Max, sliding open

Rivet's back panel. Bright blue light burst out and made him blink. "Wow!" said Max. He opened his eyes a crack and took out the glowing Skull of Thallos. The three fragments – a jawbone, eye-sockets and beak – were magically fused together. Each piece had pointed the way to the next, but they'd never glowed this brightly before.

"We must be really close," said Lia.

"I don't understand," said Max. "There's nothing around—"

A deep rumble from the seabed drowned his words and he felt the water pulse. "What in the seven seas is that?" he asked, quickly stowing away the Skull.

"I don't know," said Lia, "but I don't think we should stay here. Spike!"

The ocean shook again.

"Go up!" Lia cried. "Quickly!"

Max gasped as a crack opened in the

seabed – a huge black ring of broken
sand, running all around them. There
was another rumble and a whirring sound
as two enormous glass curved walls rose

from the ocean floor. Before they had time to move, the glass snapped shut over their heads like a giant eyelid.

On the other side of the shield, Spike swam frantically back and forth, knocking against the prison wall with his sword. Inside Rivet barked wildly, then lowered his head and set his propellers to full throttle. He charged at the glass, but bounced off with a dull clang. The fishing droid sank back through the water dizzily.

"Hard, Max," said the dogbot.

Lia swam to the line where the two halves of the dome met and Max followed her on his aquabike. There was a faint ridge at the join, but he couldn't get his fingers in to prise them apart. The dome had to be at least a hand-span thick.

Lia slammed her fist against the glass.

"We're trapped!" she said.

CHAPTER TWO

THE BLACK CAVES

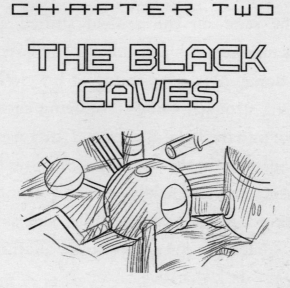

The Professor... It had to be him who had trapped them.

Rivet sniffed at the glass, following it all the way down to the seabed.

Nothing down there but sand and rocks, thought Max. But his dogbot started barking madly. At the same moment, Max felt a tug at his clothes, as if they'd been snatched by a strong wind.

"Uh-oh," said Lia.

The sand on the seabed shifted and split, opening a black hole at the base of the dome. Max felt the tug at his clothes getting stronger. They were being sucked down into the hole! By instinct, he gunned the aquabike in the opposite direction. But the suction became stronger and stronger, pulling him towards the hole. Unless he did something fast, he would plummet into the dark chasm.

Max spotted a boulder lodged in the sand at the very edge of the dome, and steered his bike towards it. With one hand he grabbed hold of the rock. With the other, he pulled the harpoon gun free from its harness.

The aquabike shot from underneath him. Max clung onto the rock, watching his bike spin toward the hole in the sea bed, then disappear underneath.

"Grab hold of my belt!" he called to Lia.

She clawed her way through the water towards him, her hair streaming along her back, clothes flattened by the power of the sucking water. She hooked her fingers around his waist. Rivet's tail propellers whined in the powerful current, trying to reach them.

With a gasp of effort, Max hooked the

harpoon gun over the top of the boulder, holding each end to lodge himself in place.

"Hold on!" he said to Lia.

She still gripped his belt tightly. "I'm not going anywhere!"

Rivet's legs scrabbled desperately in the water.

"Swim harder!" Max said. "Full throttle!"

The dogbot managed to nose forward, then dropped back, his eyes flashing with panic. He pushed again, trying to keep himself from following the aquabike, but Max could see it was hopeless.

"I'm slipping!" Lia shouted.

"Me too!" Max replied. It felt like his arms were being tugged from their sockets, and he could feel the harpoon gun creaking under the strain. He wondered which would break first.

Rivet's tail propeller stuttered and

jammed. With an electronic howl, the dogbot streaked backwards and disappeared into the hole.

"No!" Max cried. Half a second later, the fingertips of his left hand slid off the harpoon gun handle, and he was snatched by the current.

Lia screamed as the water dragged them both across the seabed. They plunged into darkness.

Max had no idea which way was up and which was down. Lia let go of his belt. He felt water whip past his body as he rolled over and over, trying to keep one hand on the harpoon gun. The back of his head slammed into a hard surface, but he gritted his teeth against the pain. Where was Rivet? Lia?

Then he was being pulled sideways by the current, sliding along instead of falling.

He caught flashes of Lia, curled into a ball just ahead. Suddenly they emerged from the darkness into dim half-light.

They were shooting along a transparent tube over an underwater canyon. Below, through his dizziness, he saw brighter lights. The suction had gone, and Max let the gentle current carry him along. He moved his arms and legs, checking for broken bones – but he'd been lucky. Lia's tunic was torn, and her eyes were wide with shock, but she looked unharmed too. Rivet's eyes had gone crossed. He shook his head, and they went back to normal.

Max's breath caught in his throat as he realised what he was looking at below the tube. Buildings and bubble-domes of all different sizes littered the seabed. But this was no Merryn city sculpted from corals and rocks. The domes had metal hatches. Pipework and cables linked them and electric searchlights swept across the landscape. Other lights flashed and valves hissed open and closed. Giant pincers on metal arms gripped and extended, lifting metal crates or huge coils of cable from one dome to the next. This was hi-tech – more advanced than anything Max had seen even in Aquora City.

Max spotted one set of claws that had got hold of his aquabike. As he watched, the robotic fist closed around it.

"No!" he yelled, but there was nothing he could do. With a crunch of metal, his beloved bike was reduced to scrap.

The tube suddenly dipped, tipping Max onto his front and carrying him steeply down into the canyon. He tumbled over again and made out shapes moving within the domes and buildings. *People!* He peered

closer. In one dome, several Merryn were treading water, shaping something out of a sea plant. In another two humans were at work with blowtorches on a piece of machinery. Some domes must be air-filled and others water-filled, Max realised. More robots scurried this way and that.

"Factories," he said, in wonder.

Lia was floating ahead of him down the tube, her nose pressed to the side. "More like a prison," she said. "I think we've found the Black Caves."

Max spotted what looked like an entrance halfway up the opposite side of the canyon – a circular metal door, big enough for a Robobeast, set into the rock and reached by a sloping walkway. Dozens of metal bolts, each as thick as his leg, locked it in place.

The Professor obviously didn't want anyone sneaking in there uninvited.

Well, we're here now, thought Max. *Even if it's not exactly the entrance I hoped for.*

Above the door loomed a giant dark screen, even bigger than the doorway and visible to everyone in the canyon below.

"I hope Spike's all right," said Lia. "He's stuck up there on his… *Aargh!*"

In an instant, she and Rivet were sucked through a hole in the side of the tube, into a smaller side-tube. A hatch slammed shut over the hole, cutting them off from Max. The dogbot's legs scrabbled but there was nothing to grip onto. Helpless, Max watched them slide down towards a large cage on the seabed that looked as though it was made of glass.

"Look out!" Max called. He tried to jam the harpoon tip into the edge of the metal hatch to prise it open, but it wouldn't budge. And now he was being tugged onwards by the current, down the main tube towards a massive water-filled dome in the centre of the canyon, below the reinforced main entrance.

With a mechanical whir, another hatch slid open and Max tumbled into the dome. He righted himself in a stream of bubbles. The dome was gigantic, but apart from him, it was empty. A pair of metal double doors at its base looked securely closed. What now?

"Max!" shouted a muffled voice.

He peered around to get his bearings and spotted Lia and Rivet in their cage just outside the dome. He swam towards them, but once again, thick glass stood in the way. They were trapped, they were separated, and they were completely at the Professor's mercy.

"Welcome, Max," said a booming voice. "Nice of you to join me."

The words seemed to come from all

around, but Max caught a glimpse of movement up above. A huge metal throne, glinting and flashing with lights, descended

through the canyon. Bubble jets hissed from built-in thrusters on every side, controlled by a man seated in its centre. A man that Max recognised. He wore a lightweight advanced underwater suit. A network of ultra-thin wires spread over the webbing that hugged his figure like a second skin. His left hand was mechanical, with long metal fingers. Max wondered if it was a glove, or a replacement for a lost limb.

"Allow me to introduce myself," said the man. "I am the Professor."

Fear seeped through Max's bones. He could hardly draw breath into his gills.

The throne hovered in the water on the other side of the dome, so that just a few inches of glass separated their faces. The Professor's mouth twisted into a smile below the visor of his helmet. "Aren't you going to say hello to your uncle?" he asked.

CHAPTER THREE

FAMILY REUNION

"Where's my dad?"

The Professor tapped the side of his nose. "In time, Max. In time."

Lia was staring at Max. "You know the Professor?" she called.

Max nodded. "He's my uncle."

He couldn't remember the last time he'd met his uncle in the flesh, but he recognised the face from holophotos his dad kept in their apartment. In those photos his uncle Dedrick had been smiling kindly at the dinner table, or standing at the water's edge in his diving gear.

There wasn't a trace of kindness in his features now. All that remained in those chilly blue eyes was arrogance and cruelty. His once-brown hair was grey. But the most surprising changes of all were the gently opening and closing gills on his neck.

"It all makes sense now," said Max. "I couldn't work out how the Professor had the DiveLog from the *Leaping Dolphin*. But of course, you were on board with my mum all along." Max slammed a fist against the side of the dome. "Let me out of here now, and release my father!"

From the cage, Max heard Rivet growl, "Bad man, Max!"

The Professor shook his head. "I admire your spirit, Max," he said, "but you're hardly in a position to make demands. The way I see it, you have a choice. Join me, or die."

"Don't listen to him," Lia called.

Max looked up at his friend, trapped with Rivet, her eyes wide, her webbed fingers wrapped around the glass bars.

The Professor frowned and switched to human language. "I shouldn't pay any attention to that girl," he said. "Without the Skull of Thallos, the Merryn are no more powerful than plankton."

"That's because you stole it!" Max shouted.

The Professor shrugged. "The choice is yours, Max. Come and work with your Uncle Dedrick. Together we can rule the oceans with a steel fist. You've shown you understand technology, like your father. I've only just started here. We can build an army – unstoppable machines to seize power not only under water, but above it too. People will bow at our feet—"

"Enough!" said Max. "I don't want any of that. I want you to give back the final piece of the Skull, and I want to see my dad!"

The Professor sighed and rolled his eyes. "Just like your mother. Last chance, Max. Will you join me?"

"You must have water blocking your ears," said Max. "I'd rather drown."

"Oh, it will be worse than that," said his uncle. He pressed a button on the armrest of his throne, and a microphone arced up in front of his chest. "Release Kraya the Blood Shark!" he cried.

Max saw the huge screen on the canyon wall flicker, glowing bright. Hundreds of other monitors dotted around the Black Caves blinked on, all showing the same image – Max floating in the water-filled dome. "What's going on?" he demanded.

The Professor flicked a switch on his throne, and suddenly his voice was amplified. "If you won't join me, I'll have to make an example of you," he said.

With a clang, the metal doors at the base of the dome slid open. All Max saw below was blackness. But then an enormous red shape rose from the depths. Max pressed himself against the glass in terror.

Kraya!

Rising towards him was the biggest shark he'd ever seen, bigger even than the largest Aquoran submarine, the X5000 Emperor Battlesub. The creature was bright scarlet from the blunt tip of its nose to its powerful tail. Only its saw-blade teeth shone white against gums the colour of blood. Cabling had been embedded in its flesh and green eyes sat high on its head. The metal doors

closed behind the predator. Max was alone
with the Robobeast.

The Professor chuckled and steered his
throne towards the cage holding Lia and Rivet.

"Let him go!" shouted Lia.

The Professor hovered directly above the cage. "You'd better say your goodbyes, fish-girl," he said in Merryn. Rivet barked in wild panic, throwing himself against the bars. "Rivet rescue Max! Coming, Max!"

Kraya swam in a wide circle around the dome. Now Max saw that the Professor had attached two huge blaster cannons by the creature's side fins, and two smaller blasters near its tail. He looked at the harpoon gun in his hands. He didn't want to hurt Kraya. It wasn't the shark's fault the Professor had captured it. But if it was a choice between that or being eaten alive, he knew he'd have to use his weapon.

I don't have long before it attacks, thought Max. *But how can I face a Robobeast alone?*

The Blood Shark thrust its tail from side to side, driving a powerful current through the water. The force of it caught Max and slammed him into the dome's side, rattling his teeth. He'd just steadied himself when a second wave tossed him the other way. Thankfully, he managed to keep his grip on the harpoon gun.

It's playing with me before the kill, Max realised.

Suddenly Kraya turned and swam straight at him. Max took aim, hoping the shark would veer away. It didn't. Instead the two big blaster cannons on its sides opened fire. Energy beams stabbed through the water, forcing Max to dodge out of the way.

"I'm only doing this because I have to," Max muttered. He pulled the trigger and the harpoon shot through the water, trailing bubbles. The point bounced off Kraya's skin without leaving a scratch. The

Blood Shark paused for half a second then kept swimming towards Max, its green eyes blazing.

Now Max had no weapon at all.

CHAPTER FOUR

DOME OF DEATH

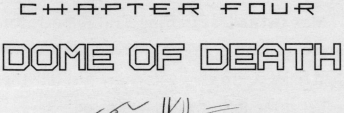

Kraya streaked through the water. When Max was within striking distance, the shark's eyes rolled back in its head, turning white.

Ready for the kill, thought Max. He kicked upwards hard. The Robobeast shot past, but its rough skin tore through Max's clothes. Max gritted his teeth at the pain as the shark's body scraped his back, and blood misted the water. Beyond the glass, he heard the harsh sound of the Professor's laughter.

Max twisted, searching Kraya's body for any sign of a robotic harness. The shark had to be controlled somehow, just like the other three Robobeasts he'd faced.

Kraya turned slowly in the water and came at him again. Again, the blaster cannons opened fire, scorching the metal floor of the dome. This time Max waited until the last minute, then used the butt of the harpoon gun to bash the Blood Shark on the nose. Kraya jerked away, but circled for another pass. *I can't keep this dodging game up forever*, Max thought. *Sooner or later, I'll tire and it will get me.*

He looked up and saw Lia watching, her face full of dismay, her fingers clutching onto the glass bars. Rivet's tail drooped between his legs. Though he couldn't see them, Max knew hundreds of prisoners must be watching too. He couldn't let them all down. He hadn't faced Cephalox, Silda and Manak, only to die now in the jaws of Kraya.

But what hope did he have against a giant, blaster-toting shark with razor-sharp teeth?

Max saw the Professor smiling, moving his throne around the dome for a better view.

He brandished the harpoon gun again as Kraya plunged towards him. He felt like a sand castle facing a tsunami, about to be swept away. Where could the harness be? It wasn't on the shark's belly, or its tail. Apart from the blasters and a few small bits of robotics, Max could see nothing on the monster's sleek red body.

Then it hit him. *If the tech isn't on the outside of the Robobeast, it must be inside!*

Which meant that to defeat Kraya, Max

was going to have to go where he'd never gone before.

Inside the monster.

Kraya paused, staring emptily at Max. Max stared back. "Come and get me, you overgrown goldfish!" he shouted.

The Professor leaned forward in his throne, knuckles white on the armrest. "Tear him to pieces, Kraya," he hissed.

The Blood Shark surged towards Max at breakneck speed. Max turned and kicked, swimming for the side of the dome. He could see Lia beyond, eyes widening, and he knew Kraya must be gaining fast.

"Look out!" Lia screamed.

"Kill him!" the Professor bellowed.

Max felt the Robobeast like a looming shadow at his back, and imagined the jaws stretching wide. He reached the dome wall, somersaulted and pushed off with his feet back the way he'd come. Sure enough Kraya was coming straight for him, teeth bared wide and glinting. Max heard Lia yell "No!" At that instant, he jammed the harpoon gun upright in the Blood Shark's gaping mouth and kicked himself into the black depths of the Robobeast's throat. Foul-smelling warm water surrounded him, but ahead he saw a faint blue glow. Max felt Kraya thrashing to spit out the lodged harpoon gun, throwing Max against the fleshy walls of its throat. He fought harder, pushing on towards the blue light.

Found it!

The harness was fastened in a ring around the inside of Kraya's gullet. And there, set into the robotics, was the final piece of the Skull of Thallos! Max grabbed onto the harness, feeling the muscles of Kraya's throat trying to suck

him deeper, into its stomach. If he let go now, a horrible death awaited – digested slowly in a living coffin. Holding on tight, Max set to work trying to find the catches with his spare hand. The blue light glowed as he tore at complex cables and circuitry. But still Kraya's body heaved left and right, up and down. Max could hardly see what he was doing, but he had to keep going...

His hand pulled something loose and suddenly the thrashing stopped. Kraya shuddered, once, twice, and gave a choking grunt. The next moment Max shot backwards with tremendous force. His body spun out, hand still clutching the harness, into the open water.

Max thumped onto the bottom of the dome prison, feeling dizzy. A few paces away the fragment of Thallos's Skull came to rest. It was the rear part of the Skull. Max scrambled towards it, and snatched it up.

I did it! he thought. *I completed my quest...*

Kraya's red bulk loomed over him. The Blood Shark bit down on the floating harpoon gun, shook it in its jaws, then crunched it to metal splinters. It spat out the pieces and turned its angry green gaze on Max.

This isn't over yet, thought Max.

With a flick of its muscular tail, Kraya swooped towards him.

CHAPTER FIVE
PLAYING CATCH

Max waited for Kraya's green eyes to roll back, then he pulled himself sideways. As the red giant streaked past, buffeting his body, Max reached out a hand and gripped the cannon above one of the shark's fins. His arm was almost torn from his shoulder socket, but he held on. Kraya yanked him through the water as fast as his aquabike. But at least he was away from those deadly teeth!

Cradling the Skull against his chest, Max

saw the Professor watching through the blur of water, right up against the side of the dome. His uncle's chest was rising and falling with excitement.

Kraya carried Max right around the edge of the prison dome. The monster's blunt nose swayed from side to side, searching for its prey. Gradually it slowed, obviously confused.

"Good work!" Lia shouted.

"Clever Max!" Rivet barked.

"You stupid fish!" shouted the Professor. Max saw him stab a button on the arm rest of his throne. There was a mechanical whir as the cannon fastenings opened and the weapon drifted free from Kraya's fins, taking Max with it.

Uh oh.

Kraya turned slowly in the water and spotted him at last.

"There's nowhere to hide now," said the Professor.

I don't understand, Max thought. *The other Robobeasts weren't interested in fighting after the harness was removed. So why is Kraya still attacking?*

And then Max saw the Blood Shark's eyes weren't focused on him at all. They were staring right at the glowing blue piece of the Skull of Thallos, tucked under his arm.

"So that's what you want," Max muttered. He held the Skull piece at arm's length. Sure enough, Kraya's nose followed. Then the monster launched forward.

Max waited until the last moment and snatched the piece of Skull back to his body. Kraya streaked past, just missing him.

The Blood Shark was just like a dogbot with a spanner... *That's it!* Max held out the Skull as Kraya circled. The shark's nose lifted, revealing its lines of teeth.

"You want this, do you?" said Max, shaking the bone fragment. He drew back his arm, shouted "Fetch!" and pretended to throw the Skull.

"Don't listen to him!" roared the Professor.

Kraya charged in the direction Max had

cast his arm, and bounced right into the wall of the glass dome. The whole structure vibrated under the impact. Kraya shook its head from side to side as if dizzy.

Cracks appeared in the dome and started to snake out. *Another impact should finish the job*, Max thought.

He drew back his arm, eyes locked on the Professor. His uncle was frantically pressing buttons on his armrest.

With a clang, the door at the base of the dome-prison swished open again and six pale glowing shapes shot out of the darkness. There was no time to lose.

"Hey, Kraya!" Max called, feigning another throw. "Go and get it!"

The Robobeast streaked towards the cracked glass, pursued by the shapes. They were attack robots, each glowing white, about the size of Max, egg-shaped with pointed tips at the front so they could move quickly through the water. Four arms trailed from each, ending in sharp grappling hooks. "Stop that shark!" screeched the Professor.

Too late. Kraya smashed into the dome, and glass exploded outwards. The Blood Shark surged through into open water.

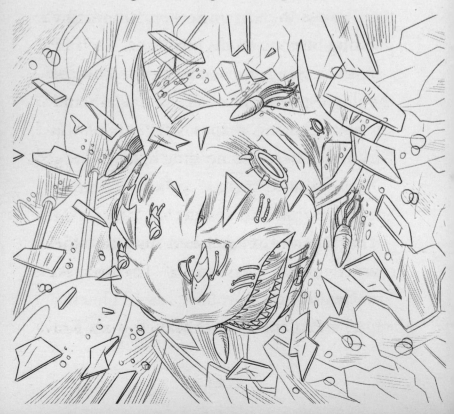

Splinters of the dome scattered in glittering shards. Max swam through in the shark's wake and dived down below a large broken section on the seabed as the deadly rain fell around him. Across the canyon, he saw the Merryn and human slaves staring open-mouthed from inside their domes. When all had settled he looked up to see the attack bots surrounding the Blood Shark outside the dome. Each time Kraya tried to move, one blocked his path, wielding its hooks. The monster circled back and forth, snapping with its jaws and batting its tail. The attack bots dodged nimbly out of reach.

It was time to rescue his friends. Max crawled out from beneath his glass shield, and shoved the piece of Thallos's skull under his belt.

The Professor's gaze turned from Kraya

to Max. His eyes narrowed with rage.

"This isn't over, nephew," he said.

He pressed another button and four metal hooks reached from the bottom of his throne. They fastened onto the top of Lia and Rivet's cage. The Professor pushed a pedal at his feet, and the hoverthrone shot upwards in a stream of bubbles, carrying Lia and Rivet with it, straight towards the circular metal door of the cavern entrance above.

A mechanical hum rang through the canyon as the door parted in the centre. Rivet howled with fear as the Professor and the cage passed through, and the entrance began to close behind them.

Max thought fast. If that door sealed, he might never see Lia or Rivet again. But if he could somehow keep it open… Max's gaze fell on one of the smaller blaster cannons which had been attached near Kraya's tail, lying among the glass fragments. He grabbed hold of it. Heaving with all his strength, he pushed off the seabed and swam towards the closing door. One of the attack bots sank through the water next to him, wires trailing from holes punched in its metal skin. Four others were busy with Kraya. The Blood Shark had one of them in its jaws, thrashing it from side to side, but blood trailed from scratches in the monster's fins.

Hang on – only four? There were six attack bots a minute ago...

Max twisted to see a pale robot stalking behind him. Its cone-head snapped open and closed, revealing circular serrated teeth, spinning fast.

CHAPTER SIX

THE PROFESSOR'S LAIR

Max's heart thumped and he kicked harder, pulling himself through the water with one hand. With the other hand he searched the blaster cannon for a trigger, but couldn't find one. The attack bot was closing fast. Max stopped swimming and prised off the rear section of the blaster. He fumbled at the circuit boards, switching wires around. If this didn't work, he was dead.

He pointed the cannon at the attack bot, closed his eyes and connected the circuit. The blaster jolted in his hands. Max opened his eyes and saw that the Professor's robot was falling towards the ocean floor, a gaping hole in its cone-head.

No time to celebrate. He had to get through those doors, find the Professor and rescue his friends.

As Max turned back, he saw that the thick metal panels of the door had almost met in the middle. Sucking water through his gills, he heaved the final few strokes and reached with the blaster, holding it out as far as he could and pushing it through the gap. The closing door clamped on either side of it, leaving a space above and below the cannon.

The mechanism made a hideous grinding sound, and the blaster began to bend. Max didn't stop to think what would happen if it snapped. He squeezed his body through the crack. The blaster bent double as Max pulled his feet through to safety. Finally it shattered, and with an echoing boom, the metal doors slammed together.

Max was lost in complete darkness. The only light came from the Skull of Thallos, glowing in his belt. If the other pieces were still in Rivet's compartment, this curved piece of bone would lead him to his friends. He pulled it out and held it loosely in his hand, then watched it swivel in his grip and gently tug to the left. *Thank you, Thallos!* Max stowed it again and swam in that direction.

Soon he reached another metal door, with a digital keypad at the side. Great! What could the code be? Max tapped in the date of his uncle's birthday – the same as his mum's. No luck. A cold chill settled on his skin. What if he was stuck in this chamber forever? He imagined his skeleton floating in the darkness. What numbers would be important to his uncle? And then he had an idea. The date of the *Leaping Dolphin*'s departure from Aquora, stamped into his head from all the holonews reports he'd read. The submarine which was supposed to carry his mother and uncle to Sumara. With shaking fingers, he typed it in.

The door opened. Max let out a long sigh of relief, and swam through.

Whoosh!

He was thrown onto the floor as water sucked past him. Then as quickly as it had begun, it was over. Max's limbs flailed and his throat tightened as he choked for breath. Then he realised what was wrong. He wasn't in water any more.

He fought down his panic and sucked air into his lungs in steady breaths. His gills closed, then another door a few feet in front of him hissed open.

"An airlock," he muttered to himself.

His legs felt wobbly as he stood up, and his whole body felt heavy after the buoyancy of the water. It was only the second time since receiving the Merryn Touch that he'd been out of the sea.

He passed shakily through the door and along the corridor, clothes dripping and soggy. Softly glowing blue lamps lit the way. *I'm so close now*, he thought. *I can't give up.*

The corridor curved upwards, and Max broke into a run. He emerged at the edge of a vast circular hall, six levels high. Five tiers of metal balconies ran around the outside, swarming with humans in white coats working at blinking consoles or checking screens. More prisoners, no doubt, and no Merryn here. But some of the men and women weren't scientists. They wore black uniforms with silver belts and collars, and carried blaster rifles. All wore Amphibio masks hanging around their necks. In case of floods, Max guessed. This had to be the main control room.

"Stubbornness must run in the family,"

boomed the Professor's voice. "You really don't give in, do you?"

One by one the scientists and guards

turned and noticed Max. He peered up towards the opposite end of the hall.

On a balcony, in front of a huge viewing window, the Professor sat in his throne. Lia knelt beside him, with her hands tied and all escape routes blocked by burly guards. Her face was covered with an old-model Amphibio mask to let her breathe out of water. Next to her stood Rivet, stationary but for his frantically wagging tail. He barked when he saw Max.

"Stuck, Max! Stuck!"

What's wrong with him? Max wondered. *Why doesn't he move?*

"Max!" shouted a voice he recognised.

Max searched the platforms and saw a man, four tiers up, gripping a handrail and leaning over. His face was pale with shock.

Max felt his heart skip a beat.

"Dad!" he yelled.

Max hadn't seen his dad since the moment Cephalox the Cyber Squid snatched him over the harbour wall in Aquora. His father looked thinner than before. He still wore his Defence Engineer's uniform, though it was torn at the shoulder and grubby.

"Guards!" the Professor barked. Two armed men on the balcony pointed their guns at Max's dad while two others grabbed his arms and pinned them behind his back.

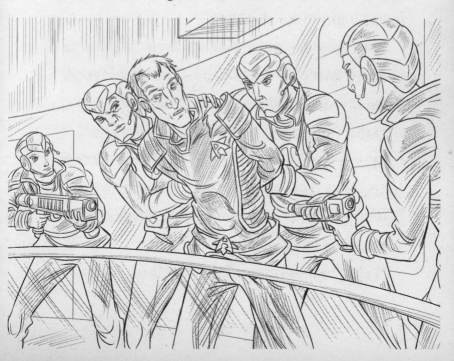

"Back to work, Callum," snapped the Professor.

Max ran up a set of metal steps, but a guard at the top levelled her rifle at his chest.

The Professor smiled grimly. "You have something I want." Max saw his uncle's gaze fix on the piece of Thallos's Skull in his belt – it was shining bright blue.

"Where are the other pieces?" said the Professor, sharply. "They must be close for it to be glowing like that."

Max had to fight not to look at Rivet's storage compartment. The curved piece of bone at his belt was glowing bluer than ever, sensing the rest of the Skull. He could feel it tugging, trying to point to the other pieces. Lia shook her head a fraction as if to say "Don't tell him!" She must have understood what was going on.

"I don't know what you're talking about,"

said Max, placing his hand over the piece of Skull.

The Professor leaned forward in his seat, face darkening. "Very well," he said. "Let's start with that bit you're holding."

Max tightened his grip. "Over my dead body."

The Professor climbed off his throne and a smile played on his lips.

"It may come to that," he said. "You may not care for your own life, but I wonder how you feel about your friend's." Max's uncle stepped past Rivet. The dogbot barked angrily, but didn't move. Max saw his paws straining and realised why he wasn't helping. The Professor must have magnetised him to the metal platform.

The Professor knelt beside Lia, and suddenly Max understood what he was about to do.

"Dedrick, no!" shouted his dad.

The Professor gripped Lia's mask under the chin. Max could see her eyes grow wide with fear.

"I'll count to five," said the Professor. "Give me the Skull, or her mask comes off."

CHAPTER SEVEN

A LIFE AND DEATH DECISION

"One!" called the Professor.

Surely even his uncle wasn't so cruel as to let Lia suffocate to death?

But if I give him this piece of Skull, he'll find the rest of it straight away and our whole quest will have been for nothing.

"Two!"

Lia tried to pull herself out of the Professor's grip. She must have known that her life was in Max's hands.

Perhaps he's bluffing…

Rivet's eyes flashed and swivelled madly. "Scared, Max!"

"Three!"

Max spotted something on the other side of the viewing window. It came close to the glass, sweeping quickly past. *Spike!* The swordfish's body whipped back and forth as he darted across the window. But there was nothing Lia's pet could do. *Even Spike can't break glass that thick.*

"Four!" said the Professor. "My patience is running out."

Max saw another shape through the viewing window, behind Spike. Something huge. Something red.

Kraya.

And suddenly, hope rose up in his heart.

"Fi—"

"OK!" Max said to the Professor. "You

can have the Skull!"

Max's uncle smiled and clicked his fingers at the woman guarding Max. "Give it to her."

Max handed the guard the piece of bone and she hurried up the ramp towards the Professor's platform. His uncle took the glowing fragment. He hadn't seen the Blood Shark yet. Max saw Kraya's green stare fix on the bit of bone. But then the monster disappeared into the black depths.

Where are you going? thought Max.

"You made the right choice," his uncle said. Then he tore the mask from Lia's face.

"No!" Max and his dad shouted in unison.

Lia fell back on the platform, choking and writhing, her bound hands clutching at her throat. Max's uncle looked sideways at the Merryn girl. Her body arched

like a beached fish.

"We had a deal," said Max, desperately. "Let her live!"

Where's Kraya?

The Professor shook his head and threw the mask across the chamber, where it landed at Max's feet. "You took all four of my Robobeasts," he said. "Did you really think I would let your friend go?"

Lia's lips were turning blue as her thrashing became weaker. Her face strained as her terrified eyes met Max's.

The Skull fragment glowed brighter than ever as the Professor held it aloft. His eyes narrowed and fell upon Rivet. "Ah… I think I've just worked out where the rest of the prize might be."

Beyond the viewing window, Max caught sight of Kraya, purple in the Skull's blue light. Just as he'd hoped, the Blood Shark was heading for the glass. The Professor wasn't paying any attention to the viewing panel though. He was moving towards Max's dogbot.

Lia stopped moving. *She can't be dead*, Max willed.

The Blood Shark's bulk grew larger all the time. Its green eyes shone with intelligence, focused on the glowing bone in the Professor's hand. Spike swam out of the way and Max tensed, ready for action.

A female guard pointed past Max's uncle

with a shaking arm. "Kr…Kray…"

As the Professor turned, the Blood Shark filled the window.

Glass exploded inwards and Max threw himself to the floor in a ball. The ocean spilled into the room in a tremendous gush. The force swept Lia off the platform and broke the magnetic hold on Rivet. The men and women on the balconies lost their footing and fell into the surging water. Through a cascade of spray, Max saw the Professor leap back onto his hoverthrone.

Max just had time to grab the Amphibio mask from the floor in front of him before the seawater flooded over him, picking him up and spinning him round. He was swept in every direction as he bounced off stairs and walls, but one thought filled his head.

Dad!

He grabbed a stair rail, righting himself. He still had the Amphibio mask, the only thing that could save his dad from drowning. He searched the bubbling, foaming flood for his father, sucking water through his gills once more. Something seized his sleeve. *Rivet!*

The dogbot dragged Max through the water. "No," said Max. "We've got to find Callum!"

And then he saw where Rivet was taking him. His dad was treading water at the top of the chamber, mouth raised into the last remaining pocket of air.

Max swam up beside him, bursting above the surface.

"Dad!" he shouted. "Put this on!"

His dad looped the mask over his face. "What about you? You won't be able to…" His eyes drifted to Max's neck and widened. "What happened to you? What did…"

The water surged over them.

Max realised his dad was staring at the

gills. He flicked a switch at the side of the Amphibio mask, turning the comms system on. "There's no time to explain," he said. "We've got to find Lia."

The control room was completely filled with water now, and they headed downwards. The other scientists and guards swam in panic towards various doors. Max was glad to see they'd all fitted their own masks in time.

Max and his dad were thrown backwards as the Professor shot past them on his hoverthrone, thrusters at full power, pursued by Kraya. The Blood Shark matched his every duck and dodge.

"Stop!" squealed the Professor. "I haven't got the Skull!"

Back at the central platform, Spike was nudging Lia's body softly with the side of his sword. Max swam quickly over and crouched beside his friend. His heart tightened. Was she dead? If she was, it would be because of him. It would be his fault.

But then he saw her gills were drifting slowly open and closed. Her eyelids fluttered.

"Max…"

He grinned as she sat up, looking around her in confusion.

"Spike saved us," said Max. "He led Kraya to the Skull. The Blood Shark goes crazy for it."

Lia threw her arms around her loyal swordfish, and he let out a series of happy clicks.

"Stop!" shouted the Professor, whizzing past with Kraya close behind. "Leave me alone!" He shot off through the wrecked viewing window and into open water.

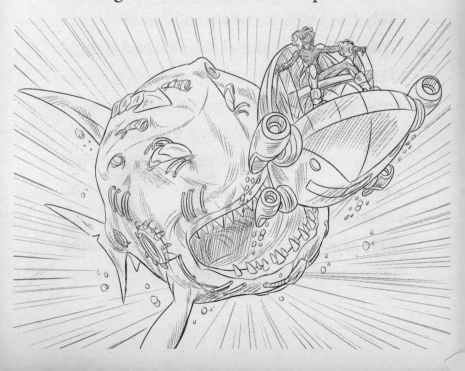

Kraya's red body streaked after him.

Lia smoothed her silver hair back from her face and pointed towards the bottom of the chamber. "Is that what Kraya's looking for?" she said. Max spotted a faint blue glow, tucked beside a control panel. His heart leapt.

"The Professor must have dropped it so the Blood Shark would stop chasing him," said his dad, laughing behind the mask. "What a shame no one told Kraya!"

Max tickled behind Rivet's metal ears. "Fetch!"

As soon as the dogbot dived, Spike raced alongside him. Both darted towards the bone fragment. Rivet got there first and tossed it up with his nose, but the swordfish snatched it out of the water and fled. Max watched as his dogbot chased Spike around the submerged control room.

"Never mind, boy," he called.

Rivet stopped, his tail between his legs, then swam back to their side. Spike followed, his mouth stretched around the bit of Thallos's Skull.

"We've got all four pieces," said Lia. "We've done it! Let's get back to Sumara and give them—"

A piercing siren cut into her words. "What's that?" asked Max.

"Five minutes to self-destruct," boomed an electronic voice.

"So Dedrick wants the last laugh," said his dad. "The whole facility is going to blow!"

"What about the prisoners back in the factories on the sea bed?" asked Max.

Max's dad frowned, his face pale under the mask. "Unless we do something fast, they're all going to die."

CHAPTER EIGHT

ESCAPE FROM THE ABYSS

"I know a shortcut back to the factories," said Max's dad.

"Then let's go!" said Max.

His dad led them out of the control room and steadily downwards through a gloomy, water-filled shaft. Max and Lia kept overtaking Callum, then waiting for him to catch up. As they swam, Max explained to Lia where they were going and what the sirens meant.

"There are Merryn prisoners there too," she said. "I can't let them die."

They reached a narrow hatch. Swimming through, they emerged at the base of the canyon. Ahead of them was the shattered dome where Max had faced Kraya.

"Four minutes to self-destruct," said the voice.

Max could see humans and Merryn trapped in factory pods and gripping each other in panic. Some were crying and others wailing with despair.

"There must be an override switch to unlock the prison chambers," said his dad. He was following a set of twisted cables along the wall.

"That's fine for the Merryn," said Max, "but if we let the humans out they'll drown. They can't reach the surface in time from this depth."

His dad used a screwdriver to lever off a metal panel set in the canyon wall. "Don't worry about them. There's another way."

The panel floated free, and his dad gripped a handful of hyper-conductors. "I hope this is right." He yanked them from the wall.

The Merryn domes hissed open and the prisoners stared at each other in disbelief.

Lia hopped onto Spike and swam above them. "Follow me!" she called down to the Merryn. "I'll lead you out of here."

Flocks of Merryn rose up from the domes, swimming after her as she climbed towards the top of the canyon.

"See you up there," yelled Lia. "And good luck!"

"Three minutes to self-destruct."

Max's dad was examining a complex set of circuit boards and switches. "Dedrick's programming is good," he muttered. "But there must be a way to release the humans too. All their chambers have escape hatches leading to the docking bay."

Max swam beside him, looking at the panel of blinking lights. "Docking bay?"

"It runs along the canyon wall," said his dad. "If we can get to it, we can use the submarines stored there to escape. Dedrick just wanted me to design weapons for him, but I did a bit of snooping too."

Max peered over his dad's shoulder at the circuitry, trying to work out how it was put together. "I think I know what to do," he said.

"Are you sure?"

Max chewed his lip. The prisoners were getting desperate, banging on the glass. He flipped two switches, avoided a third, then pressed the fourth. He eased out one of the circuit boards, and held his breath...

"Dome escape hatches open," said an electronic voice.

"Great work!" said Callum. "Those hatches will take them through passages to the docking bay. Let's go."

The human prisoners were waving their thanks and rushing to leave their domes. Max followed his dad through sliding metal doors into another airlock in the wall of the canyon. The water drained out. Max breathed air through his nose once more and his dad ripped off his mask. They stepped, soaking wet, through a second set of sliding doors and into the biggest inside space Max had ever seen. Hundreds of sleek silver vessels were stacked in hexagonal launchpods along the wall, like a giant beehive. "This must have taken years to build!" Max gasped.

"Four, to be precise," said his dad. "Your uncle was gathering an attack fleet. Just a few more weeks and he would have been ready to destroy Aquora and anything else that stood in his path."

"Two minutes to self-destruct."

The stream of frightened humans from the factory pods above piled through a far door into the bay area. "Thank you, whoever you are," said an elderly woman.

"That's Callum North, isn't it?" said a younger man in a bedraggled sea patrol uniform. "Head Defence Engineer from Aquora City."

Max felt a swell of pride.

"That's right," said his dad, climbing onto a set of loading steps. "Now listen to me, all of you. We don't have long. Find a ship and get inside. Two per vessel. If you don't know how to pilot a sub, press the

green button to activate the autopilot, and it'll navigate out of here for you."

"One minute to self-destruct."

The prisoners rushed up the steps to the tiers of vessels and climbed on board.

"Thirty seconds."

"We should go too," said Max.

They dashed up to one of the remaining subs and Max's dad pulled open the door vertically. There were two seats, side by side, and a bank of controls. As well as the basic navigation systems, Max saw buttons for torpedo launchers, laser cutters, mine-drops, grappling hooks and a host of other weapons.

"Twenty seconds."

He clambered in, and his dad took the other seat. A button brought the door down with a hiss.

"Ten seconds."

His dad's finger hovered over the red 'Launch' panel and then pressed. The sub surged forwards, throwing Max back in his seat. Narrow tunnel walls flashed past, tipped them upwards, then shot them into open ocean like a bullet.

Gradually the sub slowed and Max gained control. He steered the vessel full-circle, marvelling at the hundreds of subs floating in the water like silver pollen. The canyon wall was pocked with the round dark holes of the launch tunnels. Among the subs swam the escaped Merryn prisoners, herded by Lia on Spike. Rivet swam excitedly in front of their submarine's viewing panel.

BOOM!

The whole ocean seemed to shake, and Max felt his bones vibrate. The sea-floor below shifted and collapsed in on itself, showering rocks and plant-life down into a vast chasm. Huge clouds of sand rose from the Professor's imploding lair.

Max punched the air. "Yes! Years of work
down the plughole."

Suddenly the small screen on the sub's dashboard blinked into life, showing the Professor's snarling face. Beyond him was what looked like the inside of another submarine. *So he escaped from Kraya*, Max thought. He felt his heart sink.

"This battle isn't over, Max," said his uncle. "Especially if you want to see your mother again."

His words hit Max like a fist to the stomach. "Mum?" he said.

"Niobe?" said his dad at the same time.

The Professor's leer widened and the screen blinked off.

"He's bluffing," said his dad angrily. "Your mum is gone. He's just trying to hurt us."

How can you be so sure? thought Max.

Lia swam up to the viewing panel on

Spike and pointed upwards. "Look!" she shouted.

Max lifted the sub's nose and saw a sleek white vessel streaking away over the lip of the canyon at incredible speed.

"It must be Dedrick," said his dad.

"We have to go after him!" said Max, thumbing the thrusters.

His dad laid a palm on his hand. "There's no point," he said. "These subs couldn't keep up. That's a Nebula X-Series, Max. Fastest submarine I know of."

"But he said that Mum—"

"Son," said his dad. "Don't listen to his twisted words. We have to accept it – she's gone."

Max slumped back in his seat.

"Let's get back to Sumara," said Lia, through the sub's speakers.

Max watched the Professor's sub become

a distant dot, then disappear. It was gone.
And with it went any chance he had of
learning the truth about his mum.

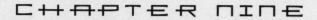

CHAPTER NINE

FAREWELLS

King Salinus sat on his white bone throne in his pearl crown, looking every inch a king.

Hundreds of Merryn were packed into the throne room, lining up between the curled coral columns to witness their return. Lia wore a silky dress of vivid green, and stood beside Max looking like a true princess of Sumara. Spike hovered in the water just behind his mistress, his sword decorated in a spiral of scarlet seaweed. Max's dad stood on his other side. A Deepsuit 2000, retrieved from the Merryn scrapyard, allowed him to breathe and kept him from floating up and away.

"Today three heroes stand before us," said King Salinus. The crowd cheered, and Rivet barked. Spike waggled his sword back and forth. "Perhaps I should say five heroes."

The assembled Merryn laughed.

"If you had told me a year ago that two Breathers would be the saviours of Sumara, I would not have believed you," said the King. "For too long we have viewed Breathers with suspicion, but Max and his father have proved themselves our allies."

The Merryn cheered once more, and Max glanced at his father. He couldn't understand exactly what was being said, but he seemed to get the gist and waved to the crowd.

"And I must also thank my daughter, Lia," added the King. "She has acted with great courage and helped bring back to Sumara our most valuable possession." An attendant carried forward the three fused pieces of the Skull of Thallos on a golden platter and offered it to the King. Lia held out the final piece – the rear part of the Skull retrieved from Kraya's throat harness. King Salinus took it and positioned it on the Skull.

A blinding blue flash brought a gasp from the crowd and Max had to shield his eyes for a second. When he managed to look again, he saw the Skull was complete and whole, as if it had never been broken. And that wasn't all that had changed. The palace walls sparkled with thousands of glittering crystal points and the colours of the wall-hangings, fashioned from weed and coral, seemed to glow brighter than before. Max felt a strange sense of calm flow through his body, as if some hidden power was laying a soothing hand on his heart. At the palace's tall windows, fish of every shape and colour hovered, looking in as if bewitched.

The Merryn Aqua Powers have been restored, he thought. *The underwater world is in harmony again.*

The King stood up from the throne and swam to the empty plinth in the middle of the room. Max noticed he stood taller than before and the wrinkles in his skin had smoothed away. He placed the Skull of Thallos in its rightful place.

"Go forth!" he called to the Merryn. "Tonight we will feast and celebrate!"

The crowd cheered, waving banners of bright seaweed, and began to file out of the palace chamber. Max's dad was carried along with the crowd, and Rivet trailed excitedly after with Spike. Soon only the King remained with Max and Lia.

"Come closer," he said.

They swam to the throne, and the King placed a hand on each of their shoulders. "You risked your lives for Sumara. You defeated the Professor's terrible creatures and liberated our people. You brought back the Skull that protects us."

Max lowered his eyes. "We failed to capture the Professor though."

"The Merryn will always have enemies," said the King. "And next time we will be more careful."

He placed a hand inside his ceremonial robes and drew out two glittering silver clasps studded with pearls. He fastened one to each of their chests.

"These are Pearls of Honour, awarded for hundreds of years to Merryn who have done their city proud."

Max swallowed. "But I'm not a Merryn."

"In your heart, and ours, you are," said the King. "The Pearls are filled with ancient Aqua Powers. With them you can summon creatures of the sea to your aid, wherever you are."

"Thank you, Father," said Lia, fingering the delicate clasp.

Max thanked him too.

"Now go and join the celebrations," said the King.

They bowed and left the throne room. Max was sure his skin was flushing bright red. He couldn't believe he deserved such an honour.

A curtain of weeds hung across the entrance to the palace. As Lia pushed it aside, Max noticed her wince.

"What's the matter?" he asked.

Lia's face was pale as she rubbed her arm. "It's nothing," she said.

Max raised his eyebrows. "Don't tell me that," he said. "That's where Manak the Silent Predator stung you, isn't it? Let me see."

Lia rolled her eyes and drew back her tunic from her arm. Max saw at once that the black bruising around the puncture wound had spread beyond her elbow.

"It's not healing properly," he said. "You need to see a doctor."

Max waited outside the healer's coral home, a short swim from the city. The King and Lia had been inside for some time. *I hope she's all right*, he thought.

His worries were interrupted by the purr of an engine, and he turned to see his dad pull up on a black aquabike with orange flashes along the side. He was towing another bike, this one sleek and electric blue.

"Where'd you get those?" asked Max.

His dad gave the black aquabike a pat. "I had a rummage through the scrapyard," he said. "They needed a bit of work, but I thought you might want a replacement."

Max climbed onto the bike and ran his hands over the touchpad controls.

There were all sorts of symbols he didn't understand, but he couldn't wait to find out what they meant. "This is awesome! Thanks, Dad."

"We should probably be getting home," said his dad. "Aquora City's been without a Defence Engineer, and it's high time I got back."

"I can't leave Lia now," Max said. "She's ill."

"Of course," said his father. "Just head up to Aquora when she's better again."

Max blushed. He hadn't realised until that moment how he felt.

"Actually, Dad," he said. "I don't think I'm going back to Aquora at all."

His father stared at him for a few seconds, then a sad smile spread across his face. "You know, I thought you might say that. You've got the Merryn Touch now, after all. Is there any point in an old Breather like me trying to change your mind?"

Max jumped off the bike and hugged his father. He didn't want to say that it wasn't just because of the Merryn Touch. It was because he loved this world. Because it was filled with marvels which he'd never see from the windows of their apartment on the 523rd floor.

"It's not goodbye," Max said. "I'll come and visit you. But my place is beneath the waves now. These people need me. At least while my uncle is still out there."

Max's dad pulled away.

"But, Max," he said, "you're not still thinking about what Dedrick said about your mother, are you?"

"Of course not," Max lied.

"Good," said his dad. "Empty hopes can destroy a person, you know." For a moment, a silence fell between them.

The Merryn King stepped out of the healer's coral home, his face drawn and pale.

"Is everything all right?" asked Max.

"I hope so," said the King. "Our healer is very wise and powerful."

Max's dad held out a hand to King Salinus, who looked at it in confusion for a moment, then took it in his own webbed fingers.

"Please…keep…Max…safe," said Callum, in stilted Merryn. Max smiled. His dad was a fast learner.

The Merryn King nodded. "I wish you a safe journey home," he replied. Max translated for his father, who smiled. King Salinus ducked back inside the healer's house.

Max's dad climbed onto his aquabike, gave Max a salute, and twisted the throttle. The bike whizzed upwards, leaving a trail of bubbles in its wake.

Max felt Rivet nuzzling at his hand.

"Callum gone, Max," said the dogbot.

"I know, boy," said Max. "I'm going to miss him."

Lia came out of the cave, a smile on her face. "Let's go and join the party," she said.

Max noticed a new seaweed bandage

knotted around her arm. "Is everything all right?" he asked.

"Of course," said Lia. "Why shouldn't it be?"

Max rolled his eyes. It was just like Lia not to admit she was in pain. *Maybe I'll bug her about it later*, he thought. *After the celebrations.*

Lia climbed onto Spike, and Max swung a leg over his new aquabike's saddle. Side by side they rode back towards the city. As they got closer to the gleaming quartz-white Arch of Peace on Sumara's main avenue, rebuilt after the battle with Cephalox the Cyber Squid, they saw people swimming around busying themselves for the feast, carrying platters of underwater delicacies, and making bunting from seaweed. A group of musicians were practising a cheerful tune. Each of their instruments was made

of multi-coloured shells.

Beyond the city, Max could see the vast ocean spreading out in every direction. *If Mum's out there, even in the deepest fathoms, I'll find her.* Max made it a promise to himself – and he was determined to keep it.

In the next Sea Quest adventure, Max must face

SHREDDER
THE SPIDER DROID

Read on for an exclusive extract...

They swam together in the direction the ball had gone. Ahead, Rivet was sniffing around among the rocks and coral, hunting for the rocketball. A shoal of fish rose from a patch of kelp, disturbed by Rivet's snuffling, and darted away.

Max, Lia and Spike joined in the search. But there was no sign of the ball.

They came to a large outcrop of rocks. "It could have gone in one of the gaps between the rocks," Max said. "And if it did we'll never find it."

Is this what you're looking for? said a voice in Max's head. He started, his skin prickling at the strange feeling of hearing someone speak inside his skull. He looked up and saw a figure rising from behind the rocks. He caught his breath.

It was a boy, about Max's own age – but unlike any boy he had ever seen. He was almost transparent. Max could just see the faint, milky outline of his body. If the boy had bones, they were transparent too. A seahorse swam behind him and Max could still see its shape through him. The only solid-looking parts of the boy were the vivid green orbs of his eyes.

Max turned to Lia. "What is it?" he whispered.

She just stared at the boy, her eyes wide with alarm. Spike was slowly rotating his fins and edging backwards. Rivet stood his ground, feet planted, and gave a defiant bark.

The ghostly boy held the rocketball in his pale hand.

Here you go.

There it was again – the voice in Max's head. The ghostly boy's lips hadn't moved. He was talking to Max telepathically.

"Did you hear that?" Max said to Lia.

"I didn't hear anything," Lia said, in a tense voice. "Come on, let's go." She tugged at Max's arm.

"Why, what's the matter?" Max asked.

"It's...a Sea Ghost," Lia said.

"A ghost? You mean he's dead?"

"Of course not, don't be silly. They're not dead, just...dangerous. I've never seen one before, but my dad used to tell me stories about them. All the legends say they bring bad luck."

It's not true, said the voice in Max's head. *Please, don't listen to her. My people need your help.*

WIN AN EXCLUSIVE
GOODY BAG

In every Sea Quest book the Sea Quest logo is hidden in one of the pictures. Find the logos in books 1 – 4, make a note of which pages they appear on and go online to enter the competition at

www.seaquestbooks.co.uk

Each month we will put all of the correct entries into a draw and select one winner to receive a special Sea Quest goody bag.

You can also send your entry on a postcard to:

Sea Quest Competition, Orchard Books,
338 Euston Road, London, NW1 3BH

Don't forget to include your name and address!

GOOD LUCK

Closing Date: June 1st 2013

SERIES 2:

THE CAVERN OF GHOSTS

OUT SEPTEMBER 2013

Dive into Sea Quest
and battle four new Robobeasts!

**SHREDDER THE SPIDER DROID
STINGER THE SEA PHANTOM
CRUSHER THE CREEPING TERROR
MANGLER THE DARK MENACE**

Watch out for the BRAND NEW
Special Bumper Edition

STENGOR THE CRAB MONSTER

OUT NOVEMBER 2013

DARE YOU DIVE IN?

www.seaquestbooks.co.uk

Deep in the water lurks a new breed of Beast.

Dive into the new Sea Quest website to play games, download activities and wallpapers and read all about Robobeasts, Max, Lia, the Professor and much, much more.

Sign up to the newsletter at www.seaquestbooks.co.uk to receive exclusive extra content, members-only competitions and the most up-to-date information about Sea Quest.

DIVE INTO THIS UNDERWATER OFFER WITH

2 for 1 entry
at

Enjoy a journey of amazing discovery with this
special 2 for 1 deal!

Just cut out the voucher below and take it into your nearest
SEA LIFE centre or Sanctuary to take advantage
of this great offer.

Fancy diving beneath the sea without getting wet?

You'll come eyeball to eyeball with everything
from shrimps to sharks, and learn tons of great
stuff from SEA LIFE experts.
So go on, take the plunge and visit your
nearest SEA LIFE centre or Sanctuary soon!

Code: Sea Quest 13